Funny Bo

The Magic Words

by Anna Prokos
illustrated by Hector Borlasca

"Scram!" Scruff tells a flea family. He scratches. He kicks. But the fleas won't move.

“Shoo!” Scruff barks at the fleas. He bites. He tugs. But the fleas won’t move.

Two stray cats laugh at Scruff. "Look what the cat dragged in," one jokes.

“I’m having a rough day,” Scruff barks. “These fleas are hounding me!”

"Do you want to know the
magic words that will help
the fleas listen?" the cats ask.

"Hot dog!" says Scruff.
"I'm all ears!"

"Say *please* to the fleas," one cat says.

"And *thank you*, too," meows the other. "Those words work like magic!"

Scruff gives it a try. "Please, fleas, will you get off me?" he asks politely. "Pretty please?"

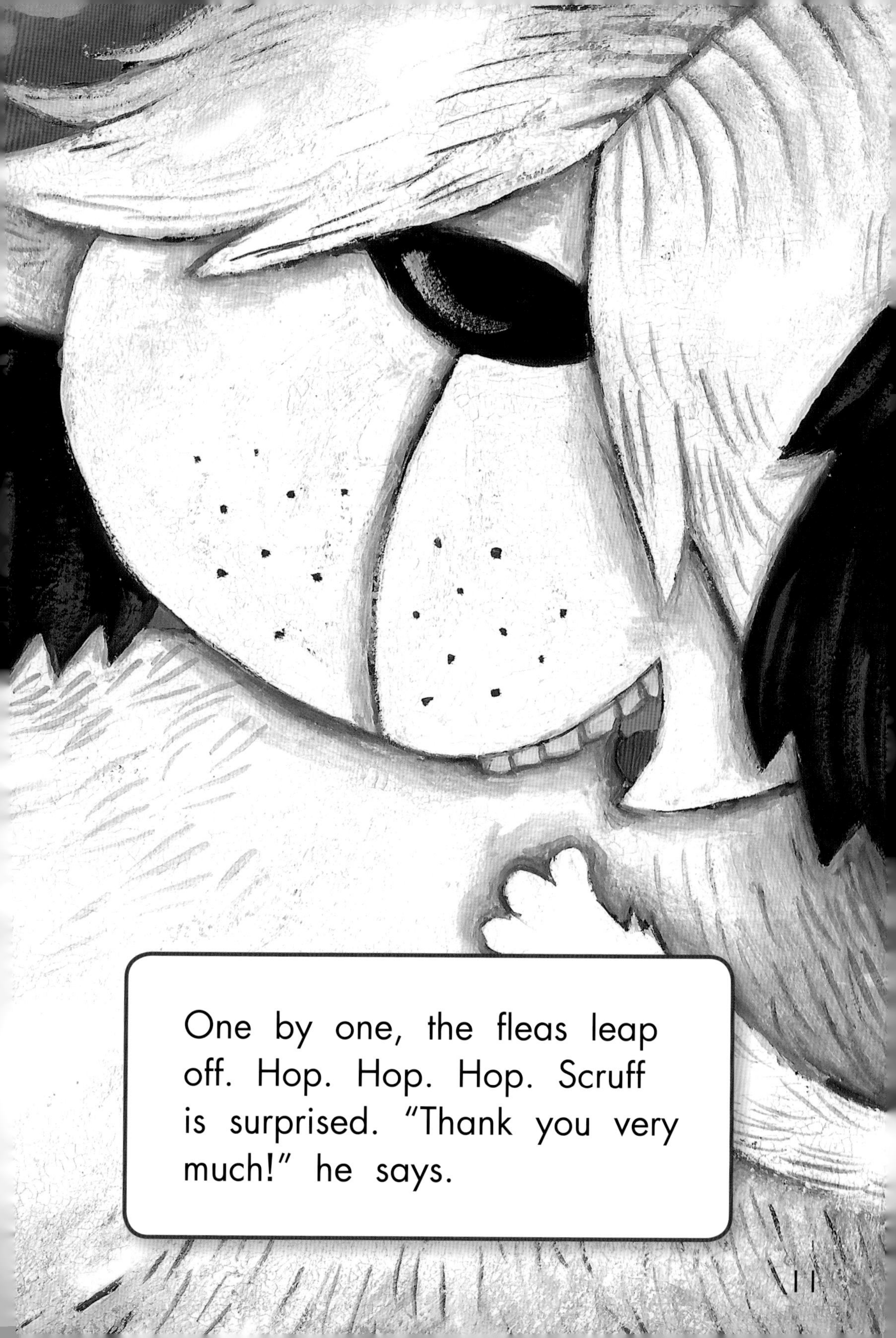

One by one, the fleas leap off. Hop. Hop. Hop. Scruff is surprised. “Thank you very much!” he says.

"That was purr-fect!"
says one cat.
"You are the cat's
meow!" the other purrs.

Scruff is proud of himself.
"Doggone it!" he howls.
"I did it!"

"Thank you for your help," Scruff tells the cats. "Those words are magic!"

The cats are pleased with Scruff. “Who says you can’t teach an old dog new tricks?” they meow.

Big Question: Why didn't the fleas move? How did Scruff finally get the fleas off of his fur? What magic words did the cats teach Scruff?

Big Words:

politely: with respect

stray: not where one should be